Praise for Let's Fall in Love 'til Wednesday

This book is for all who ever told themselves that one shot at love was enough—and then lived to change their minds. So what's wrong with throwing caution to the wind and trying a second time, as long as you make sure you just fall in love until Wednesday? Joan Wendland, the author of the acclaimed satirical novel, Alice in Corporateland, *proves that passion wasn't invented just for those under thirty or forty. The fact is, Meryl Streep, who's been around FOREVER, let an old flame into her life on her own private Greek island in* Mama Mia, *so Joan Wendland now defends the rights of all middle-aged women to dance on sandy beaches and steal a kiss at sunset. She hits above the belt, somewhere right around the heart, in this poignant and bittersweet romance set against the scenic splendor of northeastern Canada.*

Paul Davids
Producer/Writer/Director

"*I loved your book. It's honest. It's a love story I can believe in.*"

Victoria Frigo
Co-author of *You Can Help Someone Who's Grieving*

"*The landscapes, seascapes, family situations, and romantic interludes felt like a cozy quilt. Your playful writing didn't overshadow the rare quality of maturity and candidness. Remembrances of the past didn't run into sentimentality or blame. I thoroughly enjoyed your emotionally colorful and visually graphic story. Your narative drive, metaphors, imagery, and ironic situations swept me along 'til Wednesday.*"

Jim Brancaleone
Author of *Man with a Broken Heart*

Treat yourself to a lyrical journey through Newfoundland as Kate discovers falling in love until Wednesday can be a liberating experience. ...a nice combination of a romance and travelogue. ... Characters were interesting (especially her aunt) and Kate's self-revelations were marvelous.

Maris Soule
Award-winning author of romances and

Let's Fall in Love 'til Wednesday
An Adventure of the Heart

Also by Joan Wendland

Alice in Corporateland:
A Curiouser and Curiouser Bizness

Let's Fall in Love 'til Wednesday

An Adventure of the Heart

Joan Wendland

iUniverse, Inc.
Bloomington

Let's Fall in Love 'til Wednesday
An Adventure of the Heart

iUniverse books may be ordered through booksellers or by contacting:

iUniverse
1663 Liberty Drive
Bloomington, IN 47403
www.iuniverse.com
1-800-Authors (1-800-288-4677)

ISBN: 978-1-4620-2932-7 (sc)
ISBN: 978-1-4620-1213-8 (e)

Printed in the United States of America

iUniverse rev. date: 08/08/2011

To Wayne

Life is short

Art is long

Experiment is risk

Opportunity is fleeting.

—Hippocrates, 460 BCE

ive hundred miles from the top of the earth he said to me, "Let's fall in love until Wednesday." He said it while two pilot whales were surfacing off starboard and another was spouting aft when we were standing on the deck of the *Northern Princess*. The *Princess* was rust and crust around the edges and a two-hour warm, salty breeze in the face as we faced Labrador, traveling across the Straits of Belle Isle.

I hesitated, not because I dreamed of saying no. No, the hesitation was a sharp intake of breath and butterflies floating in my stomach. Butterflies he'd just said were floating in his. I said yes. How could I not say yes? I'd never fallen in love until Wednesday before, and this was Thursday and there was so little time.

They have a saying up there in the land of the Northern Lights: "Time is gettin' gone." *Aye*, I said to myself, *Kate, your time is gettin' gone*. I was celebrating my fifty-third year on this planet. The first forty were spent in saying no to life in some tight-fisted hold that consisted of doing right things, but barely a breath of life stirred for all the properness I was breathing.

Besides, he was so damned good looking, and part of the charm was he didn't know he was. Part of the charm too, was his smile. It was a new smile. A fresh smile. He'd turned a corner in life, turned life upside down, righted himself topside up, and started looking at all those ordinary things in brand-new ways ... and his smile spoke his pleasure in the looking.

Above the smile was a red mustache and above that soft, curly black hair shot with gray. And the eyes—the eyes. I never could figure out what color they really were—hazel, brown, or green. They seemed to change like the color of the seawater changes with the sun. They had warm brown flecks like soft polished amber that carried more than a glint of the rogue along with the warmth. If the eyes had achieved this, though, it was because the heart generated both.

I said yes because I'd said no to life for so long, and every no hung like a heavily weighted noose around my neck threatening to simultaneously hang and drown me. Lately the yeses were gaining ascendancy. I figured this was another yes to plug into the old balance wheel. Besides, I'd once read if you skate very fast over thin ice, you won't fall in.

It's why I'd decided in the first place to accept this gift of a trip from my parents, a whole trip on thin ice in itself. Their time was gettin' gone, as was mine. It was spring in the North Country. Chicago trapped ninety-degree days in August like a walking sauna. Besides, I was unemployed, thinned out by one of those corporate head-choppings in the personnel forest that tends to disrupt everyone's ecosystem. I was available.

The thing about familial gifts—they can tie and own you forever. Some have been so knotted and tangled that they have about strangled me. Now this added knot. How to conduct a romance under a busload of forty pairs of eyes, especially parental eyes that have looked down an inclined nose at my personal behavior?

This little romance began when I first walked down the steps of the ferry at Port aux Basques, Newfoundland. For six hours, we'd been crossing Cabot Strait from mainland Nova Scotia. I'd spent my time topside in the wind and salty air, hanging on the railing. I had pulled the scrunchie from my ponytail and let my dishwater-blonde hair play in the wind. My sneaker toes lipped out over the edge. Dots of water sprayed up off the Atlantic and collected on my jeans and windbreaker. I'd spent a wasteland of years confined to a marriage, a job, a desk, a life that now keeps me greedily grabbing for any moment, and any space, that's unconfined.

It's the childhood thing, too. Whenever I'm with my parents, I feel a great need to escape them. I escape them in my mind when I let it drift high over neighborhood health reports, the litany of restaurant meals sermonized like last suppers, and the barometric pressure on days last experienced forty years ago. That day I especially wanted to escape Mama.

"Let's sit together today, Katherine," she'd suggested that morning in that thin voice of hers that always seemed to have trouble climbing over words. I groaned inwardly. It was her birthday; I was born on her day. Katherine was fixed on me at birth and still sticks with family; anybody and everybody else calls me Kate. That morning brought the last leg of the bus trip before taking us to the ferry to Newfoundland. She'd bypassed her seat, her words invading the snug burrow I'd nestled into by to the window. Aunt Margie was jostling my elbow and tickling my mental funny bone on the other side.

Mama was such a good woman who quietly pleased everyone. I'd learned this supplication to goodness and the language of stoicism at her knee. She and I had always twisted at each other, wanting a mother-daughter closeness that could never straighten itself out in the twists. It was like we were still wrangling over my trip down the birth canal, a trip she had had induced to coincide with her day. And every year forever after I assumed a posture of gratitude for this act she had performed on her birthday.

My insides wound around resignation. As Aunt Margie's back and pack headed down the aisle to sit with Dad, my mother and her voluminous black purse pressed into the seat next to me. I pressed closer to the window.

The neighborhood report began. "The Nuggenbergers, you remember them, don't you?"

"The name, vaguely," I responded automatically.

"Well, their granddaughter just got a divorce."

"I really didn't know her, Mama."

"But you knew the family and I knew you'd want to know."

Sheila's red head bounced against the seat in front of me. She bounced around and we started bouncing philosophy, astrology, and past lives back and forth. My mother's silence and my participation seemed a fitting tradeoff to all those years I'd adjusted my life to home ec classes and typing. The first was to feed the man I was to get and the latter to support myself if he died. He didn't—die, that is, but the marriage did. "See, your mother was right," a friend said, as I began supporting myself by typing on a computer.

"No, that means that's all I prepared myself to do," I replied.

~~~ ~~~ ~~~
~~~ ~~~ ~~~

Nova Scotia floated away behind the ferry. Ahead, the rest of my mother's day loomed, along with a six-hour side-by-side ferry ride.

"I need to be out in the wind, Mama. Up on deck," I said.

"I'll just sit here and count how many people pass me," she said, her mouth pinching around the words. She smoothed her lips across her face. "You can use my jacket in case you need it." I shook my head no. Then she started coughing. She hit her doubled fist against her chest and tried to clamp the cough there.

"You need to cough it up, Mama, not stop it," I said.

"Oh, no. I can't draw attention to myself. It's just that nasty tickle I get in my throat sometimes." She strangled the cough in her chest, and then tried to push her voice through my father's two hearing aids. By the second or third repeat, her tone climbed onto its vinegary ledge.

Dad's face slid flat against the leathery lines and he sat quietly erect. He stopped the air flat between them. He had his own ledge, a harsh one that can strip to the bone. My chest constricted over this still trim and fit tree of a man carrying age rings toward his eightieth year. The land and the man, they were the same. If he could have reached the poetry of his soul, he might have said, "The dust slakes my thirst and the land quiets the rumble of my hunger." If work denied any access to the words, he sweated them from every pore. A heart attack, back surgery, and a broken hip had cooled the sweat. He worked the land quietly now, where every muscle used to spring with a tension whose sole intention was to hack the work to death.

I turned, tipped my face away from the ledges their words caught on, blurred my ears against her asking, "Did you ever notice just how many different T-shirts there are?" as I climbed the stairs to the upper decks.

Topside, I let the wind rip through and tangle my curly hair and untangle my mind. The wind was shaking damp dots of salt up off the water. I sent my mind traveling. Childhood patterns and job hunting flew in a holding pattern overhead.

Someone passed around a guitar. Everyone was singing songs of Nova Scotia and Newfoundland. Songs of land and sea, an integral part of these earth-covered rocks—especially Newfoundland, which juts above the sea in a brash dare. A dare that the sea happily pummels and pounds back along its six-thousand-mile island coast.

Then, at the bottom step, stood this handsome bus driver, looking like he belonged with the group I'd just left singing topside. He looked part Irish, part Scots, with maybe an earlier incarnation of Basque fisherman thrown in; he with the curly black hair and red mustache. I didn't know about the subtle red part mixed with the black till later, upon closer inspection. At the time I didn't know there was to be a closer inspection.

I refused the hand up the bus steps and saluted, "Hi, Neal."

"How did you know my name?" he asked, not knowing Dan, the tour director, had tipped us.

"I'm psychic," I said, rubbing the center of my forehead.

We both smiled and did some looking out of eye corners. Both pleased with the looking. *Hmm*, I mused. *Ten years since I permitted myself a flirt with a dark and handsome man.* Not that I'm prejudiced, mind you; I appreciate a nice landscape as well as the next person. But I was married to a tall, dark, and handsome empty suit for twenty years in some kind of endurance contest that could only finish in the divorce courts.

I'm tired of going someplace.

I just want to be there.

~Kate

$\mathcal{N}$eal rolled the bus out of Cornerbrook toward the Bay of Isles the next morning. Green hills spiked with stubby firs cascaded to the edge of the water. The sun tipped off the tops of the trees and cast little sparkles in the arm of water we rolled beside that rolled out to the sea.

It was a different place, but I'd been there before.You know I keep looking for a place, trying to find out where I belong. And there I was looking at another place and it was the place where I started out. When the road ended its scenic wind through tiny fishing villages and came to a stop where the arm spilled into the sea at Larch Harbor, I remembered brash cliffs along the Pacific coast; a pounding, salty spray; I remembered jumping the foamy breakers with my dad, who would swing me by my arms over the high ones.

Here it seemed time, ice, and wind had straightened out the wrinkles in the rocks. The surf was barely playing a riff, while the Pacific would have been beating kettle drums and crashing symbols. This was no endless beach where I could walk for miles, just an abbreviated hyphen, but it would have to do. While everyone else was milling around snapping cameras at seashore views and fishing boats in tucked coves, I kicked off my shoes and socks and slapped my bare feet against sand and surf. Neither time nor the beach lasted long enough, but for just a moment my feet and soul sighed happily.

As I climbed through the sand grasses and rocks to re-board the bus, I asked Dan, "Do we get any more beaches to walk on?"

His fingers combed his blond hair as if to click his mind on the itinerary. "Labrador at Blanc Sabon. It's a pretty nice stretch." Indeed. A very fine stretch.

Neal stretched out an arm to stop me. There was a tension about him that had nothing to do with stress; more like a contained electrical charge that he was figuring out how to spend. It played in his hands as he maneuvered the bus down narrow streets and open roads, and in his ready laugh with the passengers. It lighted his face when he smiled, crackled through his body, and tingled in his arm stretched to stop me. He grinned. "You don't think you're getting on my bus with your sandy feet, do you?"

"Yes." I grinned back, and tracked bare feet and sand to the back of the bus.

"It's just like when you were a little girl," Mama said with a wistful smile as I passed her seat. "You never could get enough of the sand and ocean no matter how cold it got." She and Dad had watched me through the bus window, holding onto each other as they've been doing for fifty-six years. The hold is tentative now, says life is tentative and hold on while it lasts. While it lasts, I'm bewildered over how to help them through this last rite of passage. Somehow I wish I could grab their hands and pull them up over the breakers like Dad did with me.

〰〰〰
〰〰〰

At breakfast the next morning, I was having a very sleepy start. My aunt Margie, an all-around neat lady—I mean I'd like her even if she wasn't a relative—is my roomie, and it seems she snores. Even with earplugs, my sleep was fitful last night.

We were a rolling meal of family reunions. Six of us this reunion, down a dozen or so from the larger group that flies into the Washington farm for Christmas every five years or so. The Washington and Montana clan picked me up in Chicago for the swing into Canada for two weeks.

We're a good-natured, easy-going group. We've always adopted that attitude, anyway. Any roilings to the contrary we keep under the surface, a tribute to the fine art of pretense we've practiced over the years. If conversation defaults to using weather reports as a substitute for any emotional pulse, it's easy-going talk I put half an ear to while riding my own internal waves of creative juices. Every snippet of an object, every snatch of conversation is a writing possibility—one that was impossible in childhood.

There we were, clanking our cups and silver against the restaurant crockery; I was enjoying the quaintness of the turn-of-the-century Glyn Mill Inn, silently thanking the planners-that-be for not booking us at one of the plastic chains. Then I noticed Neal at one of the window tables in front of us, and I realized I was enjoying him framed in the window, too.

I suddenly realized something. "That was you last night at dinner in the white polo shirt with Dan," I called over to him. "I thought you were a local friend of his. I didn't recognize you with your clothes on." I really hadn't intended to say it in just that way; it just popped out. Give me one nice landscape and I think it's a loaves-and-fishes multiplication. Mind you, the royal-blue uniform around his dark good looks was a pretty scene in its own right. I blundered on, "What I really mean is, having your uniform off makes a difference."

"I think you'd better stop while you're ahead," he said with a grin that slipped just a hint of what was to come into his eyes.

Uncle Harry laughed with that chuckle of his that escapes in little pieces while the rest stays inside and he shakes all over. "Why is your face getting so red?"

Yes, why indeed? I shrugged my shoulders, got redder, and laughed with everyone else. Throwing up my hands in a rather helpless gesture, I smiled and pretended I did this all the time, saying, "I tried to conceal our relationship, but now it's out. What else can I say?"

Quite a lot, as it turned out.

Night brought Neal's unexpected invitation to walk and talk (and fuel the bus). We walked along the main street in Plum Point—minus malls, fast food strips, and traffic signals, practically minus people, houses, and traffic. Clumps of fireweed and buttercups grew among the grasses by the road. Lobster traps clumped in stacks along the water. The wet rocks extending about twenty feet into the little inlet said the tide was out. Then a trillion stars studded a black, black sky unwashed by city lights. I told Neal that was how black the sky was as a kid on the farm when we pulled our beds outside on hot summer nights. He told me about his camp in the woods near Grand Falls that had the same black bowlful of stars. Crickets clicked in the quiet night, echoing through all three places. We contemplated "God was a spaceman traveling" like in the Chris DeBurgh song, how life was really accelerated lately with all the growing we'd both been doing—and feeling pushed to do all this growing for reasons we didn't completely understand. Part of the trick of life was learning what we were to learn from all these new people and new situations. What were we to learn from each other?

The ferry ride across the Straits of Belle Isle to Labrador came the next day. I was standing on the upper deck letting the breeze blow my hair back. The sea was a deep green with just the right amount of mischievous white caps. There were no icebergs in this alley often wracked with sullen weather and mean currents. The sky was milky sun, milky blue. My brain happily replayed last night's walk and talk, wishing he'd join me at the railing and we could talk some more like that. Hardly had the wish flashed in my mind than he was there at my elbow.

That's when we began putting up the glass booth. We were in our own little world where they could see in, but weren't invited to join. It was a defense against forty pairs of googly eyes pressed around the rolling fish bowl this romance was swimming in. I remember Aunt Margie and Mama at the railing throwing a few words against the glass and feeling the words drop off and slide to the deck. I think Mama knocked once more. I vaguely remembered her faded blue eyes trying to open a door, but I turned away from them before the good-girl/bad-girl picture show could start rolling through my brain, before those eyes could fasten me to my little blue chair staring at the faded kitchen wallpaper. The two of them slid to another place on the railing.

Neal dropped both arms on the railing, turned his head sideways, and looked at me, then straightened. Between sips of coffee from the Styrofoam cup he said, "You know, when I first saw you I thought you were just too straight up. Even last night when you passed by the bus, you almost seemed afraid. But then you relaxed and everything changed."

I hooked a side of my waist into the railing toward him and replied, "I never know how to act with men anymore. Actually, I don't think I ever did know. I'm basically shy. Besides, I'd never driven with a guy in a bus to get fuel. It's another one of those things I hadn't done and needed to do before I die, like watching eagles fly. Of course, I didn't know it was one of those things I needed to do, until I did it." I grinned at him.

"Ahh, that explains your T-shirt," he said, pointing at the eagle soaring across my chest. He smiled his own smile, part warm, part tease, and there were those warm brown flecks dancing like charges from all that energy rippling underneath the skin. I wanted to see where they were going to dance, and could I dance along?

We talked for an hour and a half on the ferry ride. We stood side by side at the railing without touching, being proper in our proximity, not wanting to be proper in our proximity. There was a lilt, a tilt to his voice, a song in the talking. It was a throwback to the Irish, the Scots, and the Basques, again, but this time all blended. Clear and sweet, full of fun and the devil too, his voice was, singing love songs in my ear at the dinner theater and fishing songs on the ocean trip while the whales spouted. But there I go getting ahead of my story again.

In shorthand we traveled quickly through statuses. Both divorced, he ten months, me ten years; drying out from alcohol and drying out from dry twenty-year marriages. Two children apiece. My one-of-each lived with their dad. His daughter was with him, his son with the mother. Uncommon pain and common experiences bypassed weather report type conversation and breathed life with an immediacy that transformed perfect strangers into perfect friends.

Significant others. We both had them.

"I keep asking myself, do I really want a committed relationship again? Twenty years made me feel like I should *be* committed," I said.

He curled a shoulder in from the wind and cupped his hands around a cigarette to light it. On the exhale he answered, "I know. I think about that and think, maybe I'm just a rogue. Maybe that's just me."

"You know I'm finding each and everyone has nothing to do with anyone else. Is it realistic to expect everything from one person? But none of them would probably view it that way," I said. "I get something different from each one."

He grinned, "Maybe we'll never be satisfied with just one." Rather wistfully, he added, "I'd like to think there was someone special where you'd always be connected even when you weren't together." His arm shot left and pointed, "Look, whales." Their great bodies broke water; flippers rolled upside, and then back under. "There were two of them. Pilot whales probably."

I clapped my hands. I really felt like they were the performers and I was the audience. "This is right up there with the eagles," I said, and smiled. "I've never seen whales in the ocean before."

We scanned the water for an encore. A lone whale shot a spray of water into the sky behind us. We turned back to the railing and he said, "You know, I don't usually go for intellectual women. Something about you says you're the intellectual type."

"Well, I consider myself intelligent, but not intellectual, and I've just got a high school diploma to prove it. Besides, normally I would avoid you because you're dark and handsome. The former husband was tall, dark and handsome ... though tall you are not."

"Ah, so you've got a pulse yet," he said, and his eyes shone.

"But you're right; tall I'm not." He moved so we faced each other, the knees of my jeans almost touching the knees of his blue slacks, his cowboy boots to my sneakered toes. "I don't consider myself good looking, either."

"Have you looked in the mirror lately?"

"I know other people say so, but when I look, I don't see anything that's the same as they say."

What we could say for sure was that so many people spend their time in unhappiness, they never see the happiness. When you turn life just a bit, the view suddenly becomes brand new and you get greedy for all the new looking you're doing. It's such a high to see, really *see*, clouds in the sky; the sun opening a new day. You just want to reach out and grab hold of all the beautiful ordinariness of life, to re-experience everything.

He paused and pulled on his cigarette. "Look, I have my job to consider. I'm the bus driver and you're the tourist; but what if, when I'm off the clock at the end of the day and we're spending time together—what if I were to grab your face and kiss you, like I wanted to do last night? Would you get all straight up with me and cry improper advances?"

"I'm a consenting adult, responsible for my actions," I said. "Besides, I thought about the kissing part before you said it." As I looked him straight in the eye, I could feel a full-body smile twitching through me, matching one rippling through him.

"I like that you said that." He smiled until one long dimple creased the side of his jaw, as a palm rubbed his stomach. "That gave me butterflies."

"Butterflies about kissing me?"

"That you told me you thought about kissing me before I said I wanted to."

"I like it that you told me you got butterflies," I said, shifting my eyes away at the closeness of all this. I shifted topics, too, to the little green waves the ferry was plowing through. "This whole trip reminds me of Washington, where I grew up. We didn't live on the ocean, but we spent a lot of time there. They're some of my best memories. It's why I had to be barefoot in the sand."

"When I saw you do that, that's when I knew you had spirit." He smiled, and his eyes looked far back into me for just an instant. "How long did you live there?"

"For the first twenty-one years of my life. Now over thirty in Illinois."

His mouth dropped open at that. "You're kidding. That makes you ..."

"Fifty-three," I supplied.

"I'd have guessed forty-two, maybe forty-three. I'm forty-three."

"Thanks," I shrugged, and thought, *Maybe he's lying. Maybe his eyesight fuzzes over the cracks and fault lines in my face and the sag and droop of my tits and ass ... or maybe it doesn't matter.* And maybe I chose to believe him because I wanted to believe him.

"It's funny, when I really looked my best physically I couldn't attract much more than the Empty Suit. 'Course, I was my own case of empty, so that made us a matched set. Now when I've got all these wrinkles and sags and I really don't care anymore—well, I do care—but a part of me says, what the hell! *Now* there are all these men who find me interesting."

"It's because you're more inside," he replied with a smile that creased his whole face. "I mean, you're an attractive woman and have the neatest blue eyes, but I knew I wanted to talk with you after I overheard you say you started looking at things differently after you divorced."

I let my eyes drop to the bow of the boat, the sliding water, the breaking waves. "I did take a three-year hiatus from men until about six months ago. There was a part of me that doubted men wanted me for anything but sex. I didn't eliminate men entirely, just made good friends with a couple who I knew, without a doubt, valued me for things other than sex." I turned my face back to his.

He paused. "I'm not a hit and run," he said as he stubbed out his cigarette inside the empty coffee cup, and then took a breath. "If you'll pardon me for saying it, I'm not just interested in getting laid." He smiled with a tentative tip of the lips. His eyes spoke an accent of rogue, but there was a weary edge to the language.

I slapped a hand over my mouth, then mockingly said, "A lay is a lay is a lay."

He roared and choked on the smoke of a fresh cigarette. "I can't believe how comfortable I feel with you."

That's when he asked me to fall in love with him until Wednesday and I said yes and that's when we made an appointment to kiss on the beach at Blanc Sabon.

"When I'm on the clock and in uniform, there's no touching above or below the belt. I've got my job and mortgage to consider. Agreed?"

"Agreed."

"We have a lot to do in a short time, so I'm opening a charge account for you. I'm going to spoil you," he said and flicked ashes from his cigarette into the wind. "It also requires I be a hero."

He became one in ways that neither he, nor I, recognized at the time. He even drew my parents into their own roles as heroes in tiny, significant ways. We both bought things with the charge account that we didn't ever know we needed. The gods, fate, *something* was with us and conspired to bring about this little love affair that had so little time until Wednesday.

∼∼∼ ∼∼∼ ∼∼∼
∼∼∼ ∼∼∼ ∼∼∼

Midday, when we arrived at Blanc Sabon, the sun was glorious, and the beach a decent stretch of pale sand with the surf tumbling on it, although those nasty little black flies that abound in these latitudes were swarming and lining up for open skin and blood meal.

Like I said, the fates conspired. Actually, when I think about it, I'd like to believe it was the sprites. The sprites of the night mist who met the sprites of the ocean, and the sprites of the wind that blew away every trace of the pesky flies. I could almost hear the sprites laughing and giggling—or maybe it was just my own giddiness turned inside out at walking along the beach in the dark with this handsome, charming man and indulging myself in falling in love until Wednesday. But there I am jumping ahead again.

That afternoon Neal smoothed the bus over the seventy-mile strip of road that wound around the coves, hugging the coastal waters to Red Bay. At Red Bay the road stops and you hoof it, boat it, or snowmobile it. Newfoundland grows stubby spruce, scrubby maples, and wind-flattened tuckamore atop the rocks, a weather-stunted landscape like a large-scale zen garden. In Labrador the rocks were just that. Rocks. Moody, barren, lichen-covered stacks on a bleak landscape swept bare by harsh elements. For thousands of years the elements had been sweeping and scrubbing and likely will continue for thousands more. Mats of peat grow  cow parsnips, bakeapples, wild buttercups, and purple irises above the permafrost. For hundreds of years the Vikings and the Basques, fisherman and whalers all, had been throwing themselves on these rocks and hanging onto the edge of the water to eke out a living. The square and rectangular boxes of houses that cling to the coves like Monopoly property say they are still doing it.

We combed the beach at the Saddle Island whaling station that was a boat ride, five people at a time, off Red Bay. Neal and

I were on the first boat. We sat opposite each other. He: talking with the crew and passengers. Me: with Uncle Harry, which was reminiscent of all those childhood fishing trips with him at the tiller as we trolled through lake waters. I liked sneaking looks at Neal when he wasn't looking, catching him out of the corner of my eye looking at me out of the corner of his, both of us pretending not to see and secretly smiling that we did.

Saddle Island carried grave markers and the sea-bleached bones of early Basque whalers who hung on these rocks. We picked up shells and stones and picked bakeapples, those tart, seedy-orange berry clusters that locals bend their backs over to glean $85 a gallon and convert to jams and tarts and cheesecake.

I knew all about bending a childhood back to the sun. For me, it was over strawberry fields.

Then the boat ride back and coffee at a lone cafe by the side of the gravel road that runs on bad coffee and a sleepy clock from which they've plucked the hands.

Neal slid into the booth next to me with my mother, across from Aunt Louise and Uncle Harry. The cousins had opted for coffee instead of the boat trip. They could almost be twins. One was often mistaken for the other: same height, same silver-gray hair in a neat, tidy bun at the nape of the neck, and same thin voice. The aunt and uncle were really cousins to me, the titles some deference to age.

Aunt Louise asked Uncle Harry, "Well, how was the boat ride?"

"Would have been better if they'd let me drag a fishing line behind." And that was about the last thing I can remember hearing.

It was another glass booth situation. Faces traveled through the glass. Uncle Harry looked like he was going to erupt into chuckles at any time. I ignored the words my mother threw against the glass and let them drop off outside. All I could feel was my elbow connecting to Neal's; all I could hear were the words we tossed back and forth.

As Neal and I walked back to the bus, he said, "You know,

they know what's going on; they didn't just fall off the turnip truck."

I shrugged. "I know and don't really care. That's not true. I do care. I've cared all my life for anybody and everybody but myself. It's my turn. This is my vacation, too." The toe of my sneaker scuffed a rock that shot forward about ten feet.

I flashed back on my sister's phone call just before I'd left on the trip. "I'm sure glad it's you, not me, going with Mama and Dad."

It was one of those curious paradoxes of life. If Neal and I had been alone, there would have been this marvelous freedom. But the restriction on our freedom simultaneously freed me to be who I was with my family—not who they expected me to be.

I looked over at his profile, jabbed my elbow into his arm. A dimple creased his jaw. I said, "Actually, they *are* farmers, you know. But they have fruit farms. No turnips." We both laughed.

"You don't usually do this kind of thing, do you?"

"Nope," I said.

"That says something about me that you decided to do this with me," he replied.

"Yes, and it says something about me that I decided to do this at all."

He walked over to the center of a bed of buttercups nodding yellow smiles and picked a wild purple iris emerging from the springy peat. He handed me the long stem. Three veined petals curled back softly and exposed more purple tufts.

It had been eight years since I had received a flower from a man. Then it had been two rosebuds that stayed tight and refused to open, like the relationship.

I pressed the iris between the pages of the book I was reading and later pressed a wild rose petal for him right beside it. No one had ever given him a flower, he said, and he had never smelled the sweetness of a wild rose. I gave it to him on our last night together. But I'm running to the end before I want to get there. In the end, I really didn't want to get there at all.

∿∿ ∿∿ ∿∿
∿∿ ∿∿ ∿∿

The day ended at Blanc Sabon with that walk we'd planned. With a sky under cloud cover, the only Northern Lights we were going to see were the ones at the Northern Lights Inn where we were housed for the night. As my family and I ate dinner, Dan and Neal came by.

I looked up at them. "Why don't you join us for dinner?"

"I'm having dinner in my room with paperwork," Dan said with a weary, toothy grin.

"How about you, Neal, do you want to join us?" I asked. We hadn't really planned it that way. I could have asked him from the beginning to join us. I started to, after that.

In the beginning I was avoiding an old home place. I'd moved thirty-two years and three thousand miles away from inspections of guys around the farm dinner table. Away from admonitions like, "Keep your eyes lowered, your legs crossed, and your skirt down," to the doubled-edged, "We just want to see you happy, but I certainly expect to be a grandmother before I'm an old woman." Magically, at eighteen I was supposed to reverse the admonitions, get married, uncross the legs, flip up the skirt, and produce grandbabies.

Now just like that, an independent woman who travels to England alone and asserts herself during confrontations— me!—felt reduced to the clumsy child with perpetually scraped, bloody knees and two mismatched left hands fumbling in a right-handed world. The old, familiar feeling that things were going to go wrong sank a lead weight right down through my big toes.

However, after the table had been cleared, Neal said, "I'm going for a cigarette and a walk. Kate, want to go along?" I let out a little internal breath. We'd made it this far without censure and embarrassment. The sinking feeling was lifting.

I resisted the urge to grab Neal's arm and run. "Dear aunt and understanding roomie, what time is my curfew?"

She looked at her watch and said, "Oh, make it in by six." She winked, knowing we were on the far side of eight already.

"By the way," she added, "if you hear the phone in the morning for wake up call, it's in the drawer."

"Of course. It's the first place I would have looked." I smiled, and we both started giggling.

She straightened her face, hand on a hip. "I put the phone in the drawer because there wasn't room on the night stand."

"It makes perfect sense to me." We laughed again.

I walked out of the dining room with one breath of air between Neal's shoulders and mine.

"My aunt was like this hero to me growing up, back when girls didn't have heroes," I told Neal as we walked down the hill toward the beach. "She's tramped the world to just about every country except Russia. Anything she wants to do, she does. She's not your typical seventy-four-year-old. She downhill skis and didn't take up the sport till her sixties. Does white-water rafting and seven- and eight-mile treks in the mountains."

"I feel like calling her Aunt Maggie," he said. "It just seems to fit."

"She'd probably love it. Do it."

He did the next day. She chuckled at the back of her throat like she does all happy-like, and smiled that smile that lights up her face and travels into the roots of her short, salt-and-pepper hair. "Did my niece put you up to this?"

"It was all his idea," I said. "I just encouraged him." Then I started calling her Aunt Maggie. Like Neal said, it just seemed to fit.

∿∿ ∿∿ ∿∿
∿∿ ∿∿ ∿∿

The lack of Northern Lights, or practically any other lights for that matter, led us to a doorway spilling light and a chatty babysitter who wanted to spill more conversation than directions. We just took the directions and turned right on the path past the church to the beach. After all, there was so little time until Wednesday.

"Neal burn or wind burn?" Uncle Harry asked the next morning in the breakfast buffet line, looking at my face. My cheeks and face were red that morning. I felt it before I looked in the mirror.

I punched his shoulder affectionately. "Wind burn. I've been out walking on the beach."

"You sure you don't need some help on this?"

"I can handle this, dear uncle, all by myself." I grabbed a package of saltines and tucked them in his pocket, and then mashed my fist into them.

"I'm not so sure what you can handle," Aunt Maggie chimed in. "You know that room key you couldn't find? I found it in the outside keyhole." She laughed and dangled a key in my face.

I laughed too and got redder. I'd yelled through the shower curtain that I couldn't find my key so she should be sure to bring hers—I was heading for coffee. "Well, it didn't get lost there, did it? I could've put it in the drawer with the phone, and then you'd never have found it." God! This was a rerun of that high school morning-after-a-date-feeling: certain every eye had microscopic crystal-ball sight on absolutely every muscle move from the night before.

I plunked my plate of scrambled eggs and toast on the table across from Mama and Dad and performed good-morning salutations. I shifted myself into neutral, the gear that I'd learned accommodated their need and speed. I had forever adapted to everyone else's need and speed who drifted into my life as some supplication to my goodness. Internally, my body was crashing against three hours' sleep and last night's leftover endorphins charging from the adrenals. I rode the charge like wind surf on the thermals. I let the steam from my coffee and need for caffeine drift up behind my eyelids. Passive, polite conversation ran around the surface like it's been running for years.

I ran silent. I ran deep into a rerun of last night on the beach when we walked and talked side by side, sitting on the sand, lying in the sand on the hood of my jacket, which Neal had flipped out so my hair wouldn't get sandy when he bent down and kissed me—even though I wouldn't have minded if my hair would have gotten sandy while he kissed me. "I've wanted to do that for several days," he said.

"I really like your mustache," I said, brushing it lightly with my fingers. Then I laced them through his soft, curly hair.

"I really like your perfume," he replied as he breathed into my neck. "I keep catching it every time I'm around you."

"I like whatever you've got on too. You smell like clean fresh soap with a bunch of spices mixed in."

"You want some gum?" He held out a pack. We unwrapped sticks of gum. "I'm so self-conscious about smoker's breath. I quit, and then went back when I stopped drinking. I'd like to quit, but quitting drinking is enough at the moment."

"You'll do it when you're ready," I said. "A divorce and quitting drinking at the same time is a lot to handle. I don't usually like cigarettes, but on your tongue and lips the tobacco tastes clean and fresh." I rubbed my tongue over my lips that he put his own on again.

"Maybe your feelings about me make a difference."

And later, "We're going to feel very funny walking into the lobby with wet and sandy backsides if a wave happens to send the surf up and under us," I giggled.

We stayed like that, two dark clumps in the sand, our feet a few inches from the surf.

∼∼∼ ∼∼∼ ∼∼∼
∼∼ ∼∼∼ ∼∼∼

Chairs pulling out from the table pulled me. "I still have time before the bus pulls out," I said. "I'm going for one last walk on the beach." I coulda-woulda-shoulda asked Dad to join me. He loves walking on the beach as much as I do. The good little girl whispered, *You're being selfish,* at the same time as the adult woman selfishly hoarded the lovely head spin and spent it all on myself.

I retraced last night's steps along the beach and looked at my footprints going the other way. Soon enough. Soon enough my footprints would be going the other way. The air was exhilarating, damp and salty, the sun covered in a watery mist. All by myself I twirled in the sand, my arms outstretched like stationary windmills because it felt so lovely to fall in love until Wednesday.

I don't believe in glass slippers or happily ever after any more; the slipper is broken and there's nothing quite so broken as glass. But I don't want to live like Dad's view at the other border either. "Life is just 99 percent common, ordinary, everyday living. Better find somebody you can live with, who can live through that." I lived through that until I chose not to live through that, and would rather live alone than live through that again. There's still this rag-tag remnant of the fairy tale in me though, wanting to believe that romance and special feelings can survive the day-to-day-dailies.

I walked back up the hill to meet the bus and met a gray stubble-faced man walking down. "Isn't this an absolutely great day?" I asked.

He rubbed his whiskers, blinked, looked at me like I was daft, and said, "It's a bit damp, m'love."

Neal walked out to the bus and I saw his hair full of damp curls and wished I'd been there when he got them damp, wished I could have crawled from under his blanket, away from his warm, warm body and hadn't needed to leave last night and go to my own bed.

You know, that night I was going to be all proper and straight up as Neal puts it, and then one thing just led to another and we felt so damned good together and I said to myself, *How many more proper nevers am I going to log in the regret column?* So he spoiled me with his lovemaking and the unique quakes and aftershocks that generated along every fault line of his body. Because we were looking at life in new ways and savoring its taste and scent, it was like we let all this newness that was unfolding in our lives, unfold in this age-old act. The feelings were lovely and new and quite innocent in their way, despite the two people involved having been around the block a few times.

I reran in my head the conversation last night, talking side-by-side in bed. "Stay here and marry me."

"Yes," I said, "Yes, I will until Wednesday."

And the butterflies regrouped when he said, "I'd like to take you to my camp in the woods for a month and just stay there."

While he drove the bus that morning, I leaned my head back and fantasized about that, thinking, *I'm not sure I could do that*, yet knowing there was this yearning to do something like that before I even met him; wanting to find out if I could live there a month with him in the log cabin with water carried from a stream, catching trout and wild rabbit for food and observing wildlife and writing about nature and listening to the sounds of silence and making love and being noisy while making love, which is my nature to do, because at the Northern Lights Inn, Dan was next door, and at camp I could be as loud and free as I wanted.

At coffee break he walked over to me and said, "How does here feel?" He rubbed his folded fist over his heart.

"It feels great," I smiled.

"Mine too," he smiled back.

Sometimes the only thing

I can change

Is how I look at things.

~Kate

The *Northern Princess* ferried us back across the Straits of Belle Isle early that morning. Topside was cold, the air watery; inside were coffee, talk, and Neal. Dan drifted by the lounge. He was Neal's boss, at least for the trip, by virtue of the tour company's contract with the bus company, so we invited him to join us. At one point Neal and I turned toward each other. When I looked back, I saw Dan's seat empty.

After that, every time the bus stopped, we seemed to be where each other settled. Like Neal appearing right next to me in the sod hut at one of those stop-offs on the Viking trail along the coast of Newfoundland. I was listening to the guide explain the sod huts, thinking, *This is very cozy indeed.* He suddenly materializing next to me, standing next to me, touching arms, smoke slipping out the hole in the roof, a roaring fire making things snug and cozy, an excuse to touch arms and stand close and pretend it was close quarters, and not because we wanted to be close.

We'd do it too when he'd give the seniors a hand off the bus. The first day, I'd snapped a mock salute and said, "I can handle it myself." He told me later my attitude said I didn't need anybody for anything. I have to admit that's a defense against a lot of harsh boot-heels grinding my needs and wants into the dust. Now that I'm confident I can clothe my own back, shoe my own feet, and pay my own mortgage, I can let the defenses down a few steps at a time. It felt lovely returning the squeeze he gave my hand ... it felt mildly naughty to be carrying on this way.

Mile after mile the bus followed Viking footprints. The trees and mountains I knew and grew up with were brash, cocky youngsters that scraped clouds and demanded blue real estate, especially compared to these knee-high two-hundred-year-old trees settling their weather-blunted bones into the bedrock like wise, venerable elders.

The places and weather all blended and blurred with that place I called home, where it seemed I was always returning to find out where I really belonged. The fog was like a soft, familiar old sweater in a park whose name I couldn't remember. It shuttered the mountaintops from the camera clickers and slipped down the folds of the hills. The fjord below was glassy black aluminum that jumped into snapshots of the spruce line above. Raindrops lingered on every branch and leaf.

This fog was mystical. Where I grew up, it was a shroud that crept up the valley floor to the farm on the side hill, covering the frame house that grew out of the hill like an unpainted brown thumb. There, it entered my senses off-center. Here, I could return to its soft mysticism and poetry.

One tiny village bled into the next. They were all singing the same song—a small tune, a lone whistle.

I knew all about tiny tune towns. I grew up at a one-note crossroads. The stop sign sat like a dipstick measuring the pulse of life on the gas pump at Clarence's Garage, the old general store (it was never called anything more original than that), and life at Four Corners Tavern. You could stop at the tavern and lift a few brews or toss back a few shots and pollute your lungs on secondary smoke, before anyone knew about secondary smoke. Well, I say, _you_ could stop there, but I couldn't. Good girls didn't do that.

I lay there, a half-note by the side of the road, hoping someone would pick me up and recognize my goodness. Laid on a whole lot of roadsides, never learning to sing a whole note in my own measure. Before the divorce I was going for deification as Our Lady of the Sorrowful Virgin Martyrs when I picked myself up and started recognizing my own measure. I'd already flunked home ec, typing, and virginity. I decided to drop out of martyrdom forever.

∼∼∼ ∼∼∼ ∼∼∼
∼∼∼ ∼∼∼ ∼∼∼

The sun set; dusk settled over Labrador. We rolled beside the lumpy water of the Straits of Belle Isle and a band of clouds opened on the horizon over Blanc Sabon, which we'd left on the other side that morning. Gold and orange shot through the opening and up over and all around, seeping paler fingers toward downtown Plum Point again for the night.

Neal and I plugged a few loonies into the computerized slots at the bar. Why didn't they call the dollar coin a queenie? The flip side of the picture of the loon was the Queen of England. After drinks, we took another dark walk down a deserted main street and back. Clouds scattered the stars that winked and blinked around their cover.

"I made them give me a different room," he said as he opened the door on his single room. "I couldn't handle all that space in the cabin—two bedrooms, a kitchen, and living room. It was just too much."

"I was that way when I first divorced. I couldn't even be around homes or families," I said. I lay on my stomach in the middle of his king-sized bed, propped on elbows, wearing old blue jeans and my Coca-Cola sweatshirt. He sat upright, cross-legged beside me, in a cottony orange shirt and soft jeans. I looked up. His eyes were red streaks on white.

"You really look tired." He shrugged; I continued, "Look, I loved making love with you last night and I would love to do it again, if it works out; but that's not totally what I'm about either. You've had a twelve-hour day driving us all over Newfoundland. Why don't you let me give you a massage and do some acupressure on you? It'll relax you, and I can almost promise you a great night's sleep. Nothing kinky; I'm very professional about what I do." I wriggled my fingers under his nose.

Air whooshed from his drooped smile. "Thanks," he said, "I really didn't want to take that walk. I am tired. I'm glad you noticed." Then he bent down and kissed me gently. "But last night was not a one-time thing."

"Let's just take it from one time to the next and see how it works out," I said, ducking my head.

He peeled off his shirt and jeans and crawled into bed. "I'll probably fall asleep before you leave. Let me know when you go, though."

"I promise. I'll tuck you in and kiss you on the forehead."

"Make it the lips," he grinned at half-tilt.

As I started kneading his shoulders, he said with a catch in his voice, "She'd never reach over and touch me. Never once in twenty years. She's a really good woman; we are just not suited to each other in so many ways." The pillow muffled the sadness of years of wanting, wishing, and needing, which is the most awful sadness of all, when you realize it.

Very softly and quietly I told him, "You need to be touched. Nurturing touch should be required like breathing. The skin is one of the most neglected areas of the body. Find other women to touch you like this and it doesn't have to result in sex."

Suddenly, I minded that I was sending him off to other women, just as I was going off to other men. The minding niggled until I brushed it away. None of this had anything to do with those things said and done in the future.

"We're just passing things, right? I'm not moving to Illinois and you're not moving to Newfoundland. Right?" he asked quietly.

"Right," I said. "We just have some things to learn from each other." Reason and words didn't stop the wish for just one more time, just one more thing.

I let my fingers travel the grooves and pressure points of his body. His face relaxed and opened into sleep. Charm slid away and vulnerability took its place, a vulnerability I wanted to wrap up and say, "Aye, sweet laddie, don't ever go out into the world, 'tis not a safe place for ye." I sighed. I knew all about being wrapped in plastic from which I drew in stale, stunted air, that grew a stale, stunted life. Instead I tucked the covers around him and kissed him on the forehead. He woke slightly and turned his lips to mine and said, "You're sweet. I wish you could stay." He reached up and tucked my hair behind my ears.

"Me too. Me too," I whispered. I left a small note propped against the lamp with two Hershey's kisses supplied by the hotel maids:

> *N*
>
> *I love you 'til Wednesday.*
>
> *K*

Morning pulled up early. I rolled over to the lighted dial beside the bed: 4:30. I turned over and tried to turn sleep back on, but only got Neal on the brain and Aunt Maggie breathing deeply in the next bed. Neither stopped until our 6:30 wake-up call.

A foggy mist spread outside the window. After breakfast and before folding my legs under the bus seat again, I felt the need to put my face in the mist one more time.

My eyes caught something glittery beside the curb where the water drained. I looked down. It was a dead dragonfly, a ghost of itself with a broken head and tail section. Only the transparent wings glittering with the mist were perfect. Normally these creatures play like dive bombers flying sortie. I picked it up, resurrected it from the side of the road.

I showed Neal. "What are you going to do with it?"

"Dry it off and take it home with me," I said.

His mouth corners turned up slightly. Up and over my dragonfly collection and with a rather whimsical intimacy he said, "I did get an especially good night's sleep last night, despite the fact I woke up at 4:30 and couldn't really get back to sleep."

"I did the same thing. Woke up at 4:30, I mean." We gave little startled blinks at the sameness.

"It meant a lot to me that you noticed I was tired last night."

"Even though we have a short time together, let's make it important to say what we each need to do. Like taking a walk or not taking a walk. We've both done far too many things we didn't want to do, just felt obligated to do."

"I liked finding your note this morning," he smiled, and the way his eyes touched me was the next best thing to being touched.

$$\text{mm mm mm}$$

Neal and I had our bouts of wondering what others thought. Glass-booth residents are always vulnerable to the rock throwers, real or imagined. Me, I've been braced all my life for pursed lips, clacked tongues, and wagged fingers.

John, the accountant, said to me one day as our seats rotated across the aisle from each other, "Doesn't this cramp your style, being on a trip with your family?"

I smiled and replied, "I refuse to let it."

My concern was how we reflected on Neal's job. He worried about my family's reaction. Did I mind how we appeared to the rest of the tour? It was all braided together inside us and outside of us anyway.

I liked Neal's directness with Dan. "I find her attractive and want to spend time with her when I'm off the clock. Is there any problem with that? It's not going to interfere with my job." Dan said he didn't mind, but I was still concerned.

One particular morning I felt like I got caught with my hand in the cookie jar—and Neal was the one who was going to get slapped. I'd stayed behind to use the bus bathroom rather than doing a crossed-leg shuffle behind twenty other women in the restaurant restroom line. I was last to descend and was going to bounce down the steps. Neal leaned forward into me and a good-morning kiss that only hit air when Dan appeared on the bottom step behind Neal. We jumped apart. "Better scoot," Neal grinned.

"I'll save you a seat for lunch," I called over my shoulder. My eyebrows lifted in surprise as both Neal and Dan joined the family table for lunch. Dan had established that he was "on" so much of the tour that mealtime was a time he elected to be "off." Still, it felt like I was pulling up to yet another family table of disapproval.

"We have to behave ourselves," I said to Mama, sitting across from me, "with Dan at our table." I felt so damned stiff; I couldn't relax into comfortable conversation. I felt myself getting inwardly indignant and being prepared to talk to Dan so there was no reflection on Neal. After all, Dan couldn't have been there because he wanted to be.

Dan's grin flattened slightly as he said, "Sitting with the tour can become very complicated. Some feel you're playing favorites if you don't sit with them and give them equal time. Neal's been invited to sit with you and you asked me the other night, so I just decided to join too."

"See," Neal leaned over and whispered, "I told you he's okay with us."

Nevertheless, I turned my attention to Mama. "I broke my one at home. It's just like this one," she said, pointing at the white porcelain cream pitcher. I have trouble latching on to conversations like these, just as she has trouble boosting her voice above its faintness, born of years of disuse, of abuse, choked off in the fist of an alcoholic father. Her crisp gray bun nodded over the wholeness and brokenness of both pitchers and the coincidence that this one would appear so many miles away.

"He's really very okay about us," Neal repeated as Dan got up to do tour things. "Don't set yourself up." We got up too; lunch was over, and most of the private dining room had cleared. I needed change for a tip. When I returned to the dining room to leave a loonie by my plate, I found Neal coming to do the same thing. He walked up to me and cupped my face with his hands. "We got interrupted before," he smiled, and he kissed me with a lingering sweetness I wanted to savor, except for the looming specter of someone walking in on us. I pulled away.

"If someone walks in, what will they think? And what about your job?"

He tipped his head to the side and looked at me at an angle that matched his loopy grin. "I think they might smile and think it was very nice and be happy for us. And stop worrying about Dan. Trust me."

I unclenched my teeth and tried to let my chest expand with a clear breath.

Broken psyches and broken pitchers and the coincidence of it all so many miles away had more in common than I thought.

~~~ ~~~ ~~~
~~~ ~~~ ~~~

If I liked Neal's directness with Dan, I loved it with my dad. I was ignoring what my parents thought. I'd long ago established an off-limits policy with them about my personal life, and for the most part we'd achieved a certain uneasy peace about all this, aided by the three-thousand-mile separation. Now we were housed on a bus for ten days only a few seats apart, and Neal, in some other worldly, courtly sense felt he needed to talk to my father.

"I hope you don't mind that I'm asking your daughter out." This was one of the hero parts that I didn't realize until later. No man in my fifty-three years had ever asked permission of my father. It's not that I ever thought that I needed it or even wanted it, 'til after it was done and something nice unfolded in me and felt complete because no man had ever done that before.

Dad had been my childhood hero, and an awesome one. I could never quite measure up to this slim tree of a man. I was more than slightly afraid of this man whose biceps bunched and whose veins ran like cord lines across the top of his arms when they threw an ax into wood, cutting arm-sized slices with a single stroke on the back porch.

My father was my hero this time around, too. Ten years ago, he had shouted and filled the air with blue smoke and four-letter words and ordered me out of his house for traveling around the country with a man. This time, he said, "She's an adult. She can do whatever she wants."

"I just want to assure you, she's in good hands," Neal told my dad.

"She makes her own decisions," he said.

Neal and my father both sought to tell me this. "Just goes to show you," my dad said later, brushing the flat of his palm across his full head of nearly white hair, "what kind of a person he is that he asked me that. He's all right." Males quietly seeking my approval and each other's was another heroic part.

Well, Daddy, if you'd only known just how good those hands were, you might have said no, even at my fifty-three years of age!

I think my dad did suffer from the same syndrome in reverse that children have about their parents, finding it hard to imagine their parents having sex. Yet here I am. There my sister is. There my two children are. No immaculate conceptions. And here I am a divorced woman with a healthy libido and no vows of celibacy. Mostly I think it's that our family never learned to discuss sex up close and personal. It always happened in terms of other people.

All those admonitions about propriety, fueled by my mother's fear that her father's genes would spend themselves on her children as he spent them on too much drink in too many bars with too many women. I'd like to say to them both, "I've realized your worst fears. I have sex and really love it."

Anyway, the last night of the trip my father suggested, "Tonight let's mark the route on the maps like you wanted to do."

I was barely able to keep the smile from twitching my lips at the vision of giving up a night with Neal to mark maps in the hotel room with Dad. "We'll have time. Let's do it on the plane going back," I said.

His face closed ever so slightly and he drew himself imperceptibly more erect. It was a slight shift, but I'd spent a lifetime reading the nuances of this language and it tripped my own internal speak. *You should be spending more time with your parents. You should, you should, you should,* a locomotive on a clickety-clack track circling my brain.

"We're meeting for breakfast at eight," he said, one more time.

I unhooked the engine from the train and smiled. "I may be late."

It turned out I was only fifteen minutes late for breakfast, but not because it was my first choice to be there. In the end, which came sooner than Neal or I had planned, being in the circle of my family was better than being alone.

∿∿ ∿∿ ∿∿
∿∿ ∿∿ ∿∿

Before the end, my mother was heroic in her way, too. One of the dear little ladies, one of the Beet Queens—number seven, I think; number nine was there also (honestly there really were Beet Queens on board: when I spied their red T-shirts showing juicy red beets outlined in black and broadcasting the Beet Festival, they proudly announced in unison, pointing at each other, "We're Queens. She's number seven and I'm number nine. The festival just recognizes seniors not juniors. We have real tiaras, too!")—anyway, one of the Beet Queens, I could just see her, pursing her lips, crossing her legs, and wrinkling her forehead till her gray curls and ears all moved in tandem, said to my mother, "Don't you think you'd better have a talk with your daughter?"

"She's an adult now and can do what she wants," my mother told me she'd told her. Mama continued, "I'm just glad to see you happy and having a good time." I blinked. Sucked and stopped on an inhale, like the words were strange visitors I wanted to invite in but my breath cautiously shut the door. After I'd practiced a couple of hours inhaling and exhaling this acceptance switch she'd flipped, I slid into the bus seat next to her at coffee break.

I said, "It means a lot to me that you're being accepting of Neal and me. You know we're just having fun. I love you," and I gave her a hug.

Ten years ago she was still admonishing, "All I can say, young lady, you're going to get mighty hurt by all this." The real hurt was dying from the lack of life I was living. Afraid of living. Afraid of leaving. The post-graduate adolescent traveling around the country with the guy? The experience was over almost as soon as it began. That was just part of my resurrection process. I have to admit it does seem more absurd when a fortysomething does twentysomething things.

Another heroic part was when Neal told me that he'd confided in Warren, a member of the tour who had become a friend. Their shared recovery from alcohol formed a quick bond. Neal told him, "I'm really smitten with someone on the tour." Neal assured me he hadn't said my name, although I doubt he had to by that time. None of them had fallen off any turnip truck. Warren was a minister; his wife Muriel, a social worker. They were round people who tucked themselves around each other in a second time around for each, and settled into each other with quiet pleasure and humor. The hero part was the smitten part. No one had ever been smitten about me before, not with that exact word attached to the feeling. I didn't even know I needed someone to be smitten until he said it.

ᗯᗯ ᗯᗯ ᗯᗯ
ᗯᗯ ᗯᗯ ᗯᗯ

Heroic things to me, are not these large, grand acts of rescue. They are all the small acts of beauty and kindness, no staged flourish or power-brokered gift to manipulate some end.

I knew all about power-brokered gifts from Pritchard Anthony III. He was the marriage hero. He called himself Rich (no one dared call him Pritch) and declared himself rich when he hit six figures. I married me a fine three-piece suit, I did. No dirt under his nails. He was an accountant who kept meticulous accounts on me. I never could measure up there, either.

I dropped out of power brokering when I realized that all the things I wasn't, were no one's fault, and nobody could put inside me what wasn't there. That's when I learned to be my own hero.

No, to me the heroic things are not these large acts of rescue, but these offerings out of the sincerity of oneself and shared in the natural rhythm of life out of one's own naturalness. Like being smitten. Like asking me to fall in love until Wednesday. Like asking permission of my father and me not able to give any of it to myself, and me not knowing I needed any of it—and neither did he; he just offered it up out of the naturalness of himself.

That night we went to a dinner theater; the table next to us sent over the marinated mussels, Neal started to feed me from his fork. "I like them cooked in sea water. That's how I cook them when I dive for them. A full moon is the best time. The mussels and scallops are always fatter in the shell on a full moon." He was looking straight at me and smiling as if no one else were there. "Nobody's ever done this for you before, have they?" he asked, as he put the fork to my lips. I shook my head no and tasted the tang. The texture was a bit like a tender clam.

"What about dessert? Do you like carrot cake?"

I nodded. "It's part of my vegetarian diet. Give me the potato of fries, the tomato of ketchup, and the carrot of carrot cake." He licked the frosting from his fingers, his eyes to my eyes and fed me forkful after forkful. I stifled a laugh that came out a rather silly schoolgirl giggle and thought briefly, what do these adults around us think of our behavior? But I didn't care. With each forkful he would smile into my eyes and those brown flecks would dance in his and I was very glad I had decided to dance along.

He sang, too, along with the Elvis impersonator that night at the dinner theater. "Take my hand; take my whole life too; for I can't help falling in love with you." He sang, sweet and

Happily ever now.

~Kate

clear with more than a bit of the devil in the inflection behind the lyrics as he laced his fingers into mine, under the table. Then he pulled me up into the serpentine line that danced around the room doing the Locomotion. I hadn't done this in a very long time. I was hooked on to his waist and Aunt Maggie was hooked on to mine.

That was the second-to-last night. It seems I keep slipping into the ending all the time before it needs to be there, but then again, it was always there in my mind, every day, because I knew there would always be one more thing, just one more thing I'd want to experience. And I knew I would always wonder how it would have gone on after the end.

It seemed unusual to share so much in such a short time. It's not like we intended to do that; but there was a way he was and a way I was, seeking some truths about ourselves that we could only learn through each other before we went on, so we just let it unfold as it wanted to without even talking about letting it unfold as it wanted to.

He loved Aunt Maggie—I think almost as much as I do, and would have equaled that had he known her as long. She said his good-bye hug just about cracked her ribs.

Since we both knew he was the only one calling our room, she'd answer without listening to hear who it was. "Mazie's house of sin," she'd say. "Mazie isn't in; will Sally do?" I could hear him laughing from where I sat on the bed. They had their own repartee that didn't include me and I was quite willing to share. "Yeah, sure I'll put Sally on." She handed the phone to me.

"Bring Aunt Maggie along," he said one night. "Tell her to get out of her pajamas and come down too."

"She doesn't wear pajamas. She sleeps in the buff," I said. "But I'll make sure she's decent." We played the computerized slot machines at the bar until it closed. I never could understand odds and betting. Actually, I'd never played a slot machine. I kept punching buttons, slipping in loonies, slipping my aunt loonies, and buying her a beer, which tickled me for all the times when I was a little girl and she'd given me money and presents. My system was to push the button to stop the spin when a voice in my head said so. I won ten bucks that night, spending twice as much to get it.

Aunt Maggie headed up to our room just before Mary, the cocktail waitress, said, "The bar is closing in fifteen minutes." Neal traded turns with me on his last loonie. "He's a real gentleman," Mary said, watching us.

"That he is," I replied, "and a gentle man."

He looked at me and said, "Time to go home." Too soon, soon enough. *Too soon enough*, I thought, as he turned the key in his door. Sometimes his eyes would flash open for just an instant with such an openness that it hurt to look. Maybe it hurt to look out that way too, because in the next instant the look was gone. I never asked, but I always wondered what it meant.

That night he was sorting out the significant other. "She's really pretty. A nice woman. But, I don't know." He flipped open his wallet and spilled out receipts and business cards and flung them across the dresser. "See these. She'd ask me about each one. Where I was. Who I was with." He turned away.

I walked over and hugged his back against my front. My fingers found his, which were undoing shirt buttons. "Just take it one day at a time," I said. "Like you do in AA. Let it unfold as it wants to. Only you know what's best for you. Who's best for you." I let go and sat at the foot of the bed and untied my shoelaces.

He set his jaw. "She questions me about my relationship with my wife. I mean, I was married to my wife for twenty years. We have kids. Of course we have a relationship. She's going to have to understand." He tossed his loafers at the green stuffed chair by the mirror.

"You know," I said, "it's like this guy I'm seeing. A dear, sweet, sensitive guy. But boring ... where you, you have a sparkle and sense of fun and spontaneity that I know I want, too. It's just a different combination of energy and it really gives life to the relationship." I looked up.

His dimple deepened as he sat next to me. His open shirt flopped against his chest. He slid his bare feet across the rug. "I don't think I'm ready for a commitment like she wants." I flipped my shoe off with the opposite toe. "The guy I know is really more a friend than anything. Maybe we can just enjoy that. I've decided I want that sparkle. It really adds something neat to the life." My bare feet joined his in side-by-side rubbings. "I guess we both need to be honest about what we want."

We talked like that until the words stopped and our bodies had their own things to say. He murmured against me, "This is the way it's supposed to be. This is the way it's supposed to be." This time I met him along the quakes and fault lines and discovered a new tenderness in the passion, so deep and exquisite, I didn't know whether to laugh or cry. So I did both.

ᨆ ᨆ ᨆ
ᨆ ᨆ ᨆ

Before Wednesday came, we experienced quite a lot. Even got a glimpse of his home, a cream bungalow with red geraniums, on the bus's fly-by of his street in Grand Falls. The Exploits River splits enormous red rocks thrown on either side of its banks. The rocks pile in graduated stacks like slices of bread set on end. The water rushes and roars over all this and throws up a misty steam that led to the name Grand Falls. It's also where the Atlantic salmon swim upstream to spawn. I climbed to the top of the rocks and looked down. Neal climbed up beside me.

"There is something so hopeful about swimming home with that kind of faith, against all odds," I said. "The people at the fish ladders said our Pacific coast salmon swim upstream only once in their lifetime, while your guys do it several times before they die." I sighed through a half-smile. "One all-out effort would be enough for me."

"Shows you what endurance we have. We're a heartier lot." He winked and nudged my shoulder with his, and then grabbed my hand snugly as we climbed down the wet rocks.

We walked back toward the bus and stood over the grating that covered the fish ladders. Despite all the people milling around, the roar of the water masked our conversation. "Your home is really snug and cute," I said. "Well, at least what I saw in that fly-by glimpse. You've done a lot in ten months. It took me five years before I bought a condo."

"Saves a lot of rent money. It's two bedrooms, just enough for my daughter and me. Taking care of her keeps me on track," he said as he lit a cigarette.

We looked down. A salmon jumped a ladder, then into a bigger holding tank for release later when a group had collected.

"I'll be staying at home tonight instead of the hotel," he said. "I need to see my daughter. Check in on her. Her mother's up from Hazelcorner staying with her while I'm gone." His arms folded tight across his chest.

I forced a smile onto my lips. Over the missing-him-that-night-part that tugged against a smile of genuine respect as I stuffed my hands in jacket pockets. "It's nice that you and her mother can at least work together on something like this. My ex-husband refuses to speak to me to this day, except if he happens to pick up the phone when I call the kids."

He dropped his arms and flashed a bit of his jaunty smile, "Actually, we've come down to some kind of friendship. In some ways we get along better than we ever did. We just can't live together."

Another salmon hurled itself up and over the ladder. "A friend gave me some great advice when I divorced. She said that my divorce would be as good as my marriage. I don't know why I expected great communications after, when there wasn't any before." We turned from the ladders to each other and smiled. Inside I still clutched at remnants of sadness that echoed fresh in his face. I continued, "Both my kids wanted to live with their dad. I could understand it; after all, I was the one who wanted the change—none of them did—but that was harder on me than the divorce. Ten years later, after fits and starts of speaking and not speaking, my daughter told me just a few months ago it was the best thing I could have done. She'd said she knew her dad and I had both made mistakes, and she understood why I had to leave."

With that, it was time to leave for the hotel. More would have to wait for later.

~~~ ~~~ ~~~
~~~ ~~~ ~~~

The next morning Neal looked like he'd taken a trip down into the bare bleached-bones sadness of it all. I recognized the signs; I just didn't know what to say to him. I've got my own problems with rejection. His face was hurt, closed. The brown flecks in his eyes had all but disappeared. At coffee break, he stood, bent over the railing of the bridge we'd just crossed. Cigarette smoke trailed up from his fingers as he looked down.

It was another Kodak moment, at least for those toting them. Cameras are extra baggage for me. I stand back and absorb with the senses, then translate with pen on paper. This morning my senses had only mild interest in the water rushing over the rocks below. I let one hand trail across the top of the rail and stopped it a few feet short of him. "Do you want company?" I asked tentatively.

"Of course I want *your* company. I was hoping you'd come by so I could talk with you."

"Just checking," I said. "I thought you might want some space. Men have gotten close to me before, and then abruptly, I never see them again. Makes me very wary."

"Don't set yourself up with me. I'm not like that." Then he said, "I need you." He said it so quietly it crashed a sound barrier.

Was this a hero part, or something from the charge account ... or the spoiling part? After a while they all blurred and blended into one. No man I knew ever came down off his having-it-all-together pedestal to even say the words. I'd had a husband; lots of people need me in that old propped-up dependency that kept us leaning on each other when we both should have tried some standing on our own. But this "I need you" was born out of clean, honest feeling, and didn't require any fixing on my part ... just being there to make it easier to get through.

"I wish I could reach over and wrap you in an enormous hug. It's what I wanted to do first thing this morning."

"Do you promise later?"

"I promise." It was time to board the bus again. There were schedules to keep and road maps to follow.

That road led us to Twillingate. Quiet coves and silent streets and the old whitewashed Anglican church with the steep spire. I knelt at the bench close to the jumbled bunch of wildflowers on top of the organ. Me, the woman who doesn't like churches much anymore, doesn't like to be confined in the boxes they dictate, knelt on the hard wood dented by years of knees.

I said, "So, God, what is it I'm supposed to be doing for this man who is hurting?" I unbent creaky knees that nudged me back out to the sun, where my connections to God have been far grander under the roof of the sky. A curved sandy path led past an old cemetery of chalky, tipping slabs framed by a white picket fence. The path opened to a cove looking out to sea. I stopped.

It was another one of those homecomings. My soul drank in the quiet peace outside with thirsty gulps. I smiled with tears in my eyes, "Old friend, you've been away too long." It's one of life's mysteries, how nature does that. I've received that gift countless times, yet I'm always surprised. It must have been brewed in that primordial soup and steamed into the genes. Without searching, without asking, it is there. It was born in my childhood senses back on the farm where there was no time for listening. Now I take time for listening, but I can't always hear it in the chitty-chitty-bang-bang of the city.

I ran back and found Neal feigning interest in a basket of trinkets in the gift store. "I want to show you the quiet cove I found. I don't think it knows it needed to be found."

He nodded. "Let's go." He mustered a half-smile that was full of gratitude. His body strode with a quick charge. I stepped up my pace to match his as we walked down the path.

"Last night was pretty hard for you, huh?"

"It was a painful run-in with the wife. I have to admit I cried a bit," he said.

I could hear more tears stuck in his throat. "I'm glad you can cry. You need to do that. It's all part of the deal. The biggest part of my hurt was realizing what I never had and thought I did, then knowing I was never ever gonna have it with this person."

He just nodded. The path opened to the cove; the lichen-covered rocks jutting out around the water held the quiet in. "I wanted to show you the peace that's helped me," I added.

"My camp back in the woods does that for me—and water does. I've been thinking of diving some again." We stood, silhouetted on the peat atop a rock in front of the old cemetery. We stood, bringing the outside quiet to the inside, arms touching and fingers sneaking into each other's hands, watching the distant iceberg floating and melting into the sea. We could only hear the mumbled hum of Aunt Maggie's and Dad's conversation behind us, a lone seagull's cry overhead and the buzz of the bees in the blue vetch and deep pink wild roses around us. I picked him a wild rose petal.

"Nobody's ever given me a flower before," he said, squeezing my hand as he held the sweetness to his nose.

"Do you want me to press it for you?" He nodded and smiled. His face held a new sweetness that slid into one of my own empty spots, the one that had never had a man receive a flower from me before. As we walked back to the bus, our arms brushed lightly. "I'll press it next to the wild iris you gave me and give to you before I leave."

He smiled later when I opened the book and showed him

the progress of the pressings. We could pretend we were just sharing something to read.

∿∿ ∿∿ ∿∿
∿∿ ∿∿ ∿∿

He didn't share the boat ride out the fjord to see the bald eagles, but indirectly he became a part of that in a funny way. It was through Judy and her gravel voice. Her voice was happy—just plain happy, despite its gravel timbre. I wanted to smile whenever I heard her talk. She and her husband Bill were Texans and Texas tall, he about six-foot-five and she at his shoulder. But it was their laughter that reached inside themselves and each other and spilled out that heightened everyone around.

"Why don't you buy another roll of film?" Bill called over to Judy, then confided, "If she's occupied with taking pictures she won't get seasick." If she wasn't buying a roll of film it was another T-shirt for the grandchildren—fifteen at last count, I think.

Judy handed me her binoculars as she reloaded her camera. The boat stopped and rocked in place. We followed our guide's pointed finger. The big guy, shining white head against an almost black body, was perched on a spruce watching over its eighteen-month-old chick. The chick, nearly full-sized already, had built a scraggly pile of sticks on top of a squashed boulder near the water. The adult nest was halfway up a steep cliff, nestled among the stands of spruce staggering up the cliff. It was an artful, complex fifteen-foot stack of intertwined branches camouflaged in the spruce.

I said to Aunt Maggie, "Just like Dan promised, I got to see my eagle. Now if I were really greedy I'd say I'd like to see him fly and swoop down and catch a fish."

Our guide switched directions, pulled the boat closer to shore, and cut the motor. His young deckhand winged a fish into the water. Within seconds the adult swooped down, seven-foot wings spread. Gold talons stretched and grasped the fish all in one graceful, powerful swoop.

The yellow beak ripped and gnawed as the chick with floppy, mottled new wings flew in, screeching for lunch. The adult flew to a higher perch and the baby followed. They moved to a higher one, then a third, all the way to the top of a ledge. The chick's wings flopped to the edge, its talons too tired to hang on. It slipped backward down the rock face to a flat place where it squalled and screamed. The adult polished off the fish and stood unconcerned and steadfast, out of reach. No dependency clauses in that parent-child pair were kept past their expiration date.

The engines started back down the fjord toward the dock and the bus. Aunt Maggie and I stood at the railing in side-by-side silent reflections. Our eyes drew up and across the tree stacked cliffs.

On the farm I was on the earth, not in it. I thumped and banged against it with my work ethic, never stopping to breathe with it. There I was always panting, out of breath in a frantic work step that missed the music, the dance that is nature. I heard, but did not listen. I looked, but did not see.

I renewed my pleasure in the privilege of this looking.

I walked over to Mom and Dad and gave them both a big hug. "Just seeing this alone was worth the whole trip. Thank you."

"Now that's one more thing you've done," Mama said. "We're just glad you enjoyed it." I remembered another time she'd said that: several years ago along the beach in Washington, when I'd been flying my very first kite, which I had just bought. It had a thirty-five-foot rainbow tail and made graceful, undulating waves above the Pacific Ocean waves.

"Do you want a turn, Mama?" I'd asked.

"No, I'll just sit here and watch you," she had said from her log seat, her blue hooded jacket shielding an arthritic neck from the wind. When I pulled the kite in from its maiden voyage, she'd said, "Now that's one more thing you've done."

She knows I'm making up for lost time, and maybe part of that time is hers, too, as she sits and watches me. She's a practical, no-nonsense woman, like the Newfoundlanders who build front doors they don't use. They call them mother-in-law doors. They sit half a floor above the foundation that floats above the bedrock, with no steps. No stoop. There is a back door to be used. There is no need. With my mother, the door was there for further conversation, but there were no steps ... perhaps with this woman who sits and watches me, there was no need.

The strange thing about my mouth was that it engaged in weird juxtaposition to all those profound internal thoughts. I walked over to Judy mid-gravelly chuckle and handed her binoculars back. I blurted out, "You know, seeing these eagles is positively orgasmic."

She threw her arm around my shoulders and spread her soft Texas gravel over the words, "Just how long has it been since your divorce?" Aunt Maggie joined us. Judy pointed at me. "She's getting orgasmic over eagles." We all laughed until our insides were shaking like one of Uncle Harry's laughs.

"Odd things set her off," Aunt Maggie confirmed. "The last time was when Dan was explaining the mechanical up-and-down action of the sawmill and she leaned over and whispered, 'Is that like sex in the missionary position?' We laughed like idiots all during Dan's sawmill talk. She can really be embarrassing."

Bill wandered over and wanted in on the laughter. "Your secret's safe with me," Judy said.

But not for long. When the boat docked, I walked over to Dan and Neal waiting by the bus. "This was fantastic," I said to Dan, "just like you promised. We got to see the eagles. This part was worth the whole trip." I wrapped him in a spontaneous hug that surprised both of us. I thought, *Well, Neal's standing there and a little platonic hug wouldn't hurt for him as well, now would it?*

"So, it was pretty great, huh?" he asked.

"Orgasmic. Absolutely orgasmic," I whispered. His laugh shook against my hug.

Seat rotation put me at the back of the bus, so I was last getting off back at the hotel. Neal suggested, "Let's have dinner, just the two of us, without family, okay?"

"I'd like that." How lovely. We could sit together and look at each other and talk without interested third parties pretending to be disinterested.

"I've got to get the bus ready for tomorrow, but I'll call your room on a time. But let's go later, after everyone else is gone."

As soon as Aunt Maggie left the room, there was a knock and Neal's voice on the other side of the door. "I ran into Aunt Maggie on her way to dinner." I pulled him into the room. "Very soft and silky," he said, rubbing his hands across the slickness of my deep pink pajamas.

"Well, I was stark naked and about to jump in the shower when you knocked. It's the first thing I grabbed."

"I'll bet you have very sexy underwear."

"Not anymore. I threw all that out with a lot of other things," I said. I felt sad saying that. Like I'd thrown out a big piece of me.

The pieces of me were the real problem. I was born a bunch of body parts in boxes. I lived with my head in one box, my heart in another, and feelings and sex in two others. I should have walked around with a disclaimer: *Caution, these body parts assembled by the handicapped.* The sex part got further complicated by the marriage where I prostituted myself for a dole of his six-figure salary. Sex was the least I could do for all that he did for me.

Neal was to play a big part in reconnecting the heart part to the rest of me, but I didn't know about that until after we'd said good-bye.

His mustache nestled into my face. It had its own way about it that automatically hooked the rest of me into him and him into me. We both made these humming noises in our throats that seemed to be the voice of one long satisfied length-to-length smile, all the more satisfying away from bus-rider eyes. He brushed my lips with his once more and said, "I'll go finish my bus stuff and you shower and I'll shower and then I'll come back here and pick you up, okay? I thought we'd have a drink off the patio by the bar, and go into dinner hopefully after the tour group has emptied out of the dining room."

About an hour later we were sipping dry ginger ales under the umbrella of the patio table. There was a fine mist falling. It felt invigorating. He leaned into me and said, "You know it's really okay with me if you want an alcoholic drink. I'm really all right with it."

"I feel great without it," I said stretching my arms out from under the umbrella to catch the mist. "It used to be that I'd stuff my breath down the gin bottle every night just to cope. Aunt Maggie and I have shared a few martinis on the trip and I'll have a beer now and then, but mostly I just don't want it. I don't want alcohol to interfere with the conversation."

He smiled with a spring that matched his curly hair. "Me either. I missed a lot in the haze. Blanked out the good stuff along with the marriage stuff I didn't want to look at. I get a nice buzz just being with you."

"I'm curious," I asked, "in all this sorting out and changing you've done, has there been anything you wanted to do that you're not doing now?"

"I like working with my hands. Most anything mechanical I can do. Built my own boat and did a lot of the work at the camp and on the cabin."

Here was a man who unlocked mechanical jigsaw puzzles, solved their quirks, and made them work. Hands that knew wood and metal. Hands that cooked. Hands that picked flowers and reached out and said they needed me. I shook myself over my Achilles heel—falling in love with the potential I see in men, potential that never plays the same on the daily screen as in the rushes. The Wise Woman inside counseled, "Just enjoy the now. Just enjoy the now."

With that our table was ready. The rest of the tour group had eaten and gone. Everyone except my family and Judy and Bill, all of them seated two tables away. It was like a table of seven duennas. We might as well have had all seven of them seated between us on the carriage ride through the plaza in the old Spanish courting tradition.

"I'll bet you thought you were going to avoid us," Aunt Louise called over with a sympathetic smile, "and here we still are."

"Well, it had crossed our minds," I laughed and shrugged. Neal and I sat with stiff grins like we had to pretend something for the children's sake and we didn't want to speak about what they knew without hearing anyway.

"I feel so self-conscious," Neal groaned.

"Me too; I'm just going to try to ignore them." At that point my family left the dining room en masse, which only left Judy and Bill. We both let out half a breath.

Bill called to Neal, "That was quite a turnaround on the highway today." Neal had flipped the bus around in the middle of the Trans-Canada highway and revisited a roadside moose munching leaves. The moose patiently waited till we pulled alongside, then craned his head and rack over a shoulder straight into the cameras.

"I got a great shot of the moose," Judy added. "But I sure didn't feel all that secure when we were crosswise on the highway and I looked out and couldn't see the ground the wheels were on. Felt like we were gonna drop right off the edge of the highway."

Neal laughed and asked, "How about the eagles? Did they have the same effect on you as they had on Kate?"

"It was good for me. Bill, was it good for you?" she asked, jabbing her elbow in his side. Both started laughing. "I told him," she admitted, pointing at Bill. He laughed some more and looked back and forth between the two of us, sizing up the situation. At last they just sidled out, all tall Texas of them, saying they were going for a twirl on the slot machines.

We let out the other half of a held breath. It was so everlastingly great to have the dining room empty and just the two of us seated together, out in the open talking and touching and looking like we were on a real date. God, it was positively teenagerish. Then again, when you meet a handsome, charming man who wants to fall in love until Wednesday and you have a busload of forty chaperones that includes five relatives, one might expect a whole gamut of emotions.

"When I was looking for you in the rearview mirror, I saw you writing."

"I saw you looking. I knew you were looking at me even though your sunglasses were on. I could feel your eyes. I've had a story idea," I told him. "So I've been taking notes and writing poetry." I took out my small notebook and started thumbing through the pages. "Do you want to hear one?"

He nodded and his eyes were a mix of softness and I wasn't quite sure what, as I read,

I will remember these things I like about you
You will remember these things you like about me.
We will look for them in others and ourselves
And that is how we will take each other with us.

Does it matter where we go?

As long as we stopped and met

Along the way.

~Kate

ednesday had to appear on the itinerary. The last full day of the tour. I woke up wanting the day over, not wanting the day over. I just wanted to be past the end. Way past the end. Not at the good-bye part.

Wednesday was also my parents' fifty-sixth wedding anniversary. Dad came to breakfast minus Mama. "Your mother woke up sick. Bad cold, and she's lost her voice."

I teased him, "This is quite an anniversary. Mama's lost her voice in the night and now she's spending the day in bed, without you." He smiled and didn't say anything. I didn't know if his hearing aids weren't connecting or if he didn't want to connect personally on the implied sex thing. It's the kind of remark he would have laughed over about someone else.

"I'm going to stay behind this morning with your mother," he said.

I stayed behind that morning from the tour too, and gave her a massage and acupressure. "I'm not sure this is doing you any good, Mama, but *I* feel better."

Her beautiful silver-gray hair had escaped its tidy bun and fell in wisps and clumps against her slack face. She looked so pale, so fragile. The bones felt frail, the skin thin over them. Her time was gettin' gone. Tears welled up from my chest and kept brimming at my lids. This strong woman who never rested and was a flurry of hands and feet in motion and could always do at least twenty things at once, was content to lie in bed.

"I have to be careful about pneumonia," she wrote. Talking even in a whisper was an effort, and sitting up to write caused spasms of coughing.

"It's good you can cough it up, Mama. You need to do that. I know, I used to get pneumonia all the time and lose my voice too, but I don't anymore."

She wrote back, "What did you do?"

"I got the divorce and never had pneumonia again. I don't necessarily recommend divorce for you and Dad at this point in your lives, though," I laughed. It was my cover laugh, but I no longer wanted to cover over my unspoken words. I no longer wanted to strangle them in my chest. Neither of my parents spoke. With my mother it was too much of an effort; my dad just smiled from his chair by the window. Again, I couldn't tell if it was the smile that pretended he heard through the hearing aids or it was the automatic smile we all practiced when we didn't know what to say. My mother's chest and back heaved in more coughing spasms.

Mama wrote, "I want you to go on the whale-watching trip. I don't want you staying behind. I just want to stay in bed and sleep." Her face was firm and set, her faded blue eyes resolute above the sickness. It mattered to her that I went. Dad would stay behind.

I went to the front desk, got a doctor's appointment for her, and waved them off in a cab to the nearby clinic as I boarded the bus.

I can't remember the name of the rocky point where we stopped on our way to the whales but I do remember the clouds smudging acres of blue, rocks that sheared into the smashing, crashing water. Some of us climbed the stiff bend of the lighthouse steps. On the narrow ledge at the top of the lighthouse, Bill looked down and pointed as he said, "I think Neal's trying to get your attention."

Neal flipped alternate arms up and back at the elbows.

One thumb pointed into his chest, an index finger at me. Then both arms flexed up and out, pointing cliffside like ground crew guiding a plane to the gate. He repeated it twice just to be sure I understood. I smiled and waved and circled thumb and index finger.

Bill looked back and forth between the two of us and finally asked, "What does all that mean?"

"First he's going to the bathroom. Then when I come down out of the light house, I'll meet him below and then we'll walk out to the point over the ocean."

"Looked like clipping and offside to me, but no penalties, I hope." He winked as he folded his tall frame back down the narrow opening.

After lunch I went back to the bus to get my jacket. I had just put on fresh lipstick. As I straightened up I turned into Neal coming to meet me. He'd removed his uniform tie and had a navy and red windbreaker slung over his shoulder. He laid his mustache and lips on the lipstick and probably would have rested there a moment more since no others were on the bus, but Dan boarded close behind. "I'm staying behind to do paperwork," he called out. Then he saw the two of us standing close. "Seems the two of you have been spending a lot of time together."

"I'm writing a story about Neal. I'm doing some research," I said as I headed for the door. On the way by, I tried to rumple Dan's blond hair, but he ducked out of reach.

"Uh, before you go out, I'd wipe the lipstick off," I said to Neal. Dan smiled into the papers he was digging out of his case.

Neal and I climbed the ladder to the flying bridge of the boat. We both wanted to be closest to the sky and farthest out in the wind. The boat bumped and swayed with the swells of the Atlantic, which was a whole other excuse to let ourselves get tossed together and stand close together and then too by that time it was the last day. We tossed pretense over the side into the waves that last day and began touching like lovers do—a rub of the back, a tug of the sleeve, a squeeze, a hug, a pat—out in the open salty air. Not that we fooled ourselves that anyone was fooled before. Several people snapped pictures of us together standing there on the flying bridge looking down at them and them looking up at us. Maybe they just wanted a picture of Neal, and I happened to be standing next to him. I'd like to think it was like Neal said: maybe they just liked seeing us laughing and talking and being happy.

Humpback and minke whales were breaching, spouting water all around. "Each time they spout it's like one long satisfied sigh," I said. "Now this is the stuff of life that's really important. That started happening to me after I divorced. The car, the house, the clothes ... none of those things carried the same importance after that. I still like them and want some, just to get along. They just have a different place now."

He nodded. "I know what you mean. It's like that song that keeps running through my head. Something about wandering away farther than I should and not being able to find my way back. That's what I feel like. That I did wander away, now I've returned to life's simplicities in all kinds of ways.

"Watch that lighter shade of green just below the surface, one's about to surface." He pointed, tipping my shoulder in the direction of his point. One great humpback heaved its body completely out of the water and slipped smoothly back in, tail fin waving once, twice, three times. I could feel an enormous smile stretch all through me. I reached over and hugged Neal. It was as if these great creatures all decided to come out and play on this day, just for us.

He hugged back and said, "I love this just as much as you even though I've grown up here."

His smile was huge and stretched through both of us.

The sun was shining, the whales were breaching and spouting, Neal was singing with the music over the boat speakers, and we were enjoying this together. "These songs about the sea are so much of what Newfoundland is about," Neal said. I could feel it in his voice, the rhythm of the words and music that all matched the sway and swell and smoothness of the boat rocking on the sea as the wake fanned open behind us. A swell jostled me smoothly into the dent of his shoulder. Another pitch knocked us askew. We grabbed onto the aluminum rigging overhead and hung at arm's length and let ourselves move whichever way the sea moved the boat. "Did you know that your eyes are incredible? There's a certain way you look—maybe it's the light. I mean you're pretty, but sometimes the way you look, there's a glow."

"You know, this is like about a year ago when I laughed for the first time 'til I just about peed my pants and woke up the next morning with sore stomach muscles because I'd laughed so hard. I said, 'Now that I have laughed that hard, I can die.' Then I'd hit my forehead and said, 'Dummy, now you can laugh some more before you die.' It's like the eagles," I told him. "Positively orgasmic."

I yelled down to Judy who was buying another roll of film on the lower deck, "There are three things on this trip that have been just like the eagles. The eagles and the whales and I'll tell you the third later."

That night at the farewell dinner, I hung my arm around her shoulders. "So what's the third thing?" asked Judy.

"The eagles, the whales, and Neal. All positively orgasmic," I said.

She drawled, "Oh, my dear, when I saw him I just about went off myself! All that curly dark hair at the neck; I'd just love to run my fingers through it." I took her by the hand and Neal laughingly let her do just that.

"It's so soft, so soft," she said.

"I know. I know."

∿∿ ∿∿ ∿∿
∿∿ ∿∿ ∿∿

Before we went to dinner that night, I said to Aunt Maggie, "I need an extension on the curfew tonight. Don't leave the patio light on; I'm not coming home." She smirked as I added, "See, Neal's off the tour as of noon today. He's just hanging around for the farewell dinner. Tonight he's staying in a hotel across town where the bus company puts them up, and I'm staying with him."

At the table we saved a place for Neal between us; when he walked in, I whispered, "It's not fair that you look so good." A beige and cream woven textured sport coat, beige slacks, and a tie splashed with gold leaves and earth tones set off that smile of his and dark curly hair above.

"You do, too," he said, as his eyes scanned my white knit shirt with the lace bra that showed through. I also wore some beige woven pants held up by braces and a necklace of strands of carved bone and beads and leather falling from an abalone shell. I knew I looked good. Tanned skin, dishwater blonde hair loose and curly and lightened by my summer off in the sun. Neal's eyes reflected it all back to me just as mine were reflecting back to him.

He had to make a phone call and I left for the restroom. We converged outside the dining room at the same time. "We seem to do this a lot, be in the same place at the same time, unexpectedly," he said. Then he kissed me softly with a light brush of his mustache and said, "I loved it that you said I looked good."

"What I wanted to do then was to reach over and do exactly this," I replied, and we traded smiles again, lip to lip.

"I was afraid of six-inch heels."

"See, just like I promised," I said. "No heels. I really did throw them all away."

Shoe to shoe, we were the same height. Barefoot—well, barefoot we were still just right.

ᗰᗰ ᗰᗰ ᗰᗰ
ᗰᗰ ᗰᗰ ᗰᗰ

Good-byes, addresses, and promises to write were exchanged. All those things that seem vital at the time that are usually forgotten in the day-to-day-dailies ... it's like taking pictures as proof you've been there. I handed Dan his tip envelope: "It's been a slice," I said. "You made it a super trip." He reached over and hugged me and kissed my cheek. Neal was right; I really didn't have to worry about Dan. "You know you're not gettin' a tip from me. That would be just too weird," I told Neal. I was helping him count his tip money. We had the piles of envelopes and cash on the bed between us. A half an hour before a cab had slipped us to the other side of St. Johns, away from the historic section with the row houses stacked on the hillside to the more contemporary section of fast foods, malls, and the Best Western for the night.

"I told you," he said, "I opened a charge account for you to use however you want."

"I do have an envelope for you, though." I handed him a note; pressed between its pages was the wild rose petal I'd pressed for him.

N

When you think of me, think of wild roses and the cove at Twillingate where the lichen-covered rocks jut out over the sea, and we stood on the rock looking down, our shoulders just touching and our fingers sneaking into each other's hands and letting the silence of the cove wrap around us.

What a lovely romantic thing to do—to fall in love until Wednesday. The only thing is—how do I unfall in love on Thursday?

> *Love*
>
> *K*

As he read his face got softer and softer and his eyes the warmest I'd ever seen. That's when he said the thing I will never forget. The best gift of all in the short time I was to know him. He said, very softly, "You don't unfall in love. You don't. You don't."

At that point he swept all the money off the bed and tucked my note and the rose petal beside the lamp. The brush of his mustache was coming down easy, coming down slow, and, well—some things are private.

Except I will tell you it ended differently than either one of us thought. At one point that night, I said,"I just feel so greedy. We're never gonna be able to satisfy all the times that won't be there. I want to stop," I said. "Could I just lie here next to you until morning? Is that okay?"

He smiled and his eyes looked that way again for an instant that went very deep into himself. It hurt me to look at them like that, and then it was gone. "Very much okay," he said. "I can't imagine they'll have the bus ready much before ten anyway." He kissed me softly and we fell asleep rubbing against each other.

The next thing we knew, the phone was ringing rudely at 7:30 a.m. The bus was ready. The abruptness of all that was a wrench we didn't expect. Neal scrambled for the shower and both of us for clothes.

"You know you can stay longer; take your time," he said.

"No, I want to leave when you leave. I'm okay leaving you, but I won't be if I don't leave with you."

We tried a "sweetheart" and a "darling" apiece that seemed flat strangers in the room. In the rush, there was a kind of helplessness that hung suspended. There seemed to be so much to say, but there was no time to say all the unsaid things much less the immediate ones that couldn't find a way to be said.

"We don't need to say any more," I said.

We waited for the cab with the night clerk going off duty, who bummed cigarettes from Neal. Then he and the cab driver talked about the Trans Am that was stolen in the night and the constabulary that was out looking for the thief. Neal told him he needed to get his brakes checked.

We held hands through all of this as the cab slid across town back to my hotel. The closer it got the tighter we squeezed. "We don't need to say any more," I wanted to say once more, but the words stuck in the tears sliding around in my throat. The cab slid down the hill to the Hotel Newfoundland and up the curved drive to the front door.

His face flickered light and dark, as if trying to pull up

words from inside. "Don't forget to write," was all he could say. We kissed softly. Too softly. Too quickly. There were schedules to keep, road maps to follow. I fumbled with the door handle, my eyes blurring. "God bless," he called through the shutting door.

"God bless," I echoed and tried to rub the chill from my arms through my thick sweater. I slung my purple backpack over my shoulder, waved, and let the revolving door spit me out on the other side. The elevator slid me smoothly to my floor. My heart felt like a large smashed thumb. The door was quiet on the inside. Aunt Maggie was at breakfast.

I walked over to the window and looked down on the street the cab was traveling, taking him to the bus that was ready to roll for another tour. The sun was shining on the narrows that led out to the sea. My dragonfly was still resting on the windowsill. Next to it was a cotton-lined jewelry box and a note.

For a safe ride home.
Love, Aunt Maggie.

I split the cotton, rested the dragonfly between the layers, and tucked some soft socks around the box in my suitcase.

I threw myself face down on my unslept bed and let myself cry. "When I'm missing you, I'm going to try to remember this choice I made to enjoy you," I sobbed into the comforter.

But once you speak Stoic, there's always an accent to the language that remains. Five minutes later I got up, splashed cold water on my face, changed my clothes, grabbed my breakfast voucher, and decided to join my family. I would only be fifteen minutes late. Besides, it felt good knowing I had a family to go to.

Mama, pale and tired but with a recovered voice, felt better enough to come to breakfast. "I thought you'd be later," Aunt Maggie said.

"We did too," I replied, "but the bus was ready sooner than he thought." Then I got quiet. They did too. The back door was there, as it always had been. They are a practical, no-nonsense people—no need to use the front door.

The toast tasted like chalk. The fruit was dry. The coffee refused to jump-start me. When breakfast was over, I went to Uncle Harry. "I could really use a hug this morning," I said. He wrapped me up in one tight enough to squeeze a blur into my eyes ... or maybe they were doing that all on their own. Then he grabbed my knee like he used to do when I was a little kid to get at the funny bone and make me laugh. I smiled through the blur. Aunt Louise walked over and said, "Let me give you a hug too. I'm so glad you had a good time, but this must be real hard leaving Neal." I could only nod.

It didn't seem safe to ask my dad for a hug when neither he nor my mother were offering. Part of those old patterns, old voices. *You knew what you were getting into. No use crying over spilled milk.* There were still some needles I hadn't gotten unstuck from childhood on this trip, but a whole bunch of them I'd picked up and laid down in different grooves.

"Thanks for the box," I told Aunt Maggie when we got back to the room. "I feel like a walk, although I'm really tired. Didn't get much sleep last night."

"Don't tell me your problems," she laughed, and then her own eyes filmed over as she looked at me. I don't know how I looked but I sure was feeling a miserable jumble inside.

"I've got time before we leave for the airport."

I walked along the narrow streets, paralleling the channel that led to the narrows that led to the sea. Somebody pointed me to the path that led up the rocky hill. The wind was blowing hard off the Atlantic, but the sun was out and the deep, deep purple clover spilled down the banks in masses to meet the pools caught in the rocks. I walked along the rocky path high above the channel into the wind and did some crying into the wind. It was a clean hurt. Honest. One I couldn't begrudge myself. Not like the old days, when it was a sharp echo rising out of a huge canyon to slash jagged edges against the wrists.

And then after the crying had stopped, all of a sudden I

felt this bubbling joy that started at my toes and ran right through me out the top of my head. *You know, he's right. I don't have to unfall in love. I've had this really goofy idea about love. That it had to end when a relationship ended or when I didn't see him anymore. And that's why my heart's been so tiny. It got all constricted, skewed out of shape because I thought every time something ended that the love stopped. It was just me stopping my heart, making it tiny. That's why I've hurt so much.*

Something in my heart unfolded, something that had never ever expanded before. All the tight wrenchings and dents and pushes and pulls I'd put it through, straightened out. All the love I'd tried to stop just opened up and got very large.

Is forever more lasting?

When what we shared remains

Past the time of leaving.

~Kate

his morning I'm back in Illinois. If they made their connections, Aunt Maggie is in Montana, everyone else in Washington. The sadness lingers. I expect it will for a while, but filtering through it is a breath I haven't pulled before. I feel my heart is just learning to breathe.

I'm at my favorite rock seat by Lake Michigan, this inland sea in the Midwest that for me is a childhood facsimile of the Pacific Ocean. I come here once a day (or more) to do some serious rock sitting. No ninety-degree days to finish out August. This morning it's foggy and damp, like I brought the air with me from Newfoundland at Cape Spear where fog smudged the rocky high cliffs, while the surf crashed far below. The rocks are low here, rolled by some department of beach erosion. Just a few gentle splashings of the lake this morning.

Last night I unzipped the suitcase, left the dirty clothes where they still are this morning, and unpacked the box with the dragonfly. It made the trip safely. I mounted it on the wall in my living room under my cartoon clock that says, *Open 24 Hours—Clydes Day of Sandwiches*, and just over the Indian shield and the two baby starfish. The last were a gift from Mama in my stocking last Christmas, the stocking she made for me because red velvet stockings with white lace and jingle bells were not a part of my practical childhood.

On the plane ride back last night, Dad said, "I'm really glad you got to spend time with your mother on this trip like she does with your sister back home. Doing things you like to do together."

I took a deep breath. We were still forgiving each other's differences. You're supposed to forgive your parents. The hardest part for them has been forgiving me for being different. I'd made a choice to believe in who I was, not to be a rubber stamp of who they were, to be proof their life mattered. I'd stopped that fiction for myself; now I needed to stop it for Mama.

With a deep breath, I said, "Actually, I really _don't_ like doing some of those things. Like shopping. It really bores me. I feel bad that we don't share those interests, but I'm happy with who I am. I'm sorry, though, for your sake that there are things like that we don't share."

"People are just different," she'd sighed, her shoulders turning in around the words.

"You must take more after me," smiled Dad, sitting between us. "I don't like shopping either."

A block out on my walk this morning, a slab of sidewalk offered up yet another dead dragonfly. This one has a bright spring green body, complete with a head and tail section. The wings are soft gold, like fine vermeil, and shine in the sun. I cupped it in my hand and carried it back to my place before continuing to the lake. It will have a place on the wall next to the Newfoundland one, a "Before" and "After" still life.

From my perch on the rock, I can see a monarch butterfly emerge from the fog. It circles my head before landing on a milkweed flower for breakfast. I figure that's a good sign too. There is something so hopeful about this fragile creature that is strong enough to fly from the Midwest to Mexico to winter over.

The last thing Aunt Maggie said to me at the airport when we hugged good-bye was, "When you write to Neal, send my love." I write it on the mist this morning.

"Oh, one more thing," I whisper. "God bless."

The words travel on the mist that meets the lake waters that travel out all the great lakes to the St. Lawrence Seaway that flows to the Atlantic that splashes around that earth-covered rock that is a place in the heart, that is a place in the sea—new found land.

Acknowledgments

Friends and family all made significant contributions. My thanks to my biological family, Rob Humphrey, Jill Humphrey, George Wendland, and Nadine Wendland. Thanks too, to my adopted family, the Farrans, Fred, Ed, and Diana, for their unconditional acceptance.

Karen Nowosel, Vickie Frigo, Emma Metherell, and Paul Davids have all helped make this book possible in ways that are unique to them.

Mama Java's Café Express and the Candlelight provided low-rent unofficial office space! Special appreciation to Whitney Scott, who piloted me through this project.

About the Author

The author originally published this book after a job layoff (on April Fool's Day. No fooling!) The story idea was born from a vacation taken after that layoff and from vacation journaling. After receiving many rejection slips (the last one, after a year), the author decided she wanted a book in her hands before she died.

Armed with a high school diploma and a master's degree in life experience and without a background in publishing, sales, marketing, or advertising, she wrote, self-published, *and* had a movie option from a Golden Globe–nominated producer within six and a half months! She subsequently cowrote the screen play adaptation, having never done that either.

She was featured in the *Chicago Tribune, Today's Chicago Woman,* and *Chicago Women in Publishing.* One book does not make a writing career, so she couldn't quit the day job. Movie production was to have started in the spring of 2009, but the economy tanked and so did the project at that moment in time. Stay tuned!

After wifehood, motherhood, and a stint as *Alice in Corporateland,* she found her real 'hood: creativity. She does story performance of original stories for groups in Living Out Loud. The author resides in South Haven, Michigan, where she facilitates two creative writing groups.